PUBLIC LIBRARY DISTRICT OF COLUMBIA

W9-BUX-740

www.mascotbooks.com

Diwali: A Cultural Adventure

©2013 Sana Hoda Sood. All Rights Reserved. No part of this publication
may be reproduced, stored in a retrieval system or transmitted in any
form by any means electronic, mechanical, or photocopying, recording
or otherwise without the permission of the author.

For more information, please contact:
Mascot Books
560 Herndon Parkway #120
Herndon, VA 20170
info@mascotbooks.com

CPSIA Code: PRT0813A
ISBN-10: 1620863960
ISBN-13: 9781620863961

Printed in the United States

Diwali
A Cultural Adventure

Sana Hoda Sood
illustrated by Rubina Hoda

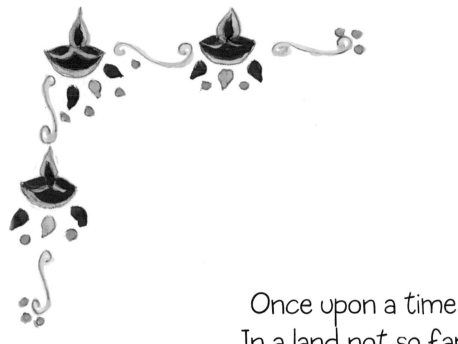

Once upon a time
In a land not so far
There lived the great King Rama
Who shone as bright as a star.

His Kingdom was in India.
His kindness loved by all.
By every man, woman, and child
By all creatures, big and small.

King Rama was so noble
With a heart made from gold.
He lived a life of honor
And loved all, young and old.

But first let's go back
To where it all did start,
When the wicked were defeated
By those who were pure of heart.

It started as a battle
But ended in delights.
The triumph of good over evil
And then the Festival of Lights.

When he was just a young prince
There came to be much strife.
Young Rama was sent to the forests
To live with his brother and wife.

Rama, Lakshmana, and Sita.
Together stayed the three
Spending fourteen years in the forests
Until an enemy brought misery.

This started an epic battle
As Rama had to find his wife.
So with the help of Hanuman and Lakshmana
He set off to save her life.

The battle was intense and magical
When Rama and Raavana finally did meet.
With Rama's courage and strength
Raavana was left in defeat.

With the celebration of his victory
And his wife once more with him,
Rama returned home from the forests
To brighten the lamps that were dim.

The Kingdom rejoiced for Rama.
He was now their King,
Their Lord, the bringer of hope.
What was quiet, could now sing.

Everyone lit up with smiles
And there was peace once more
As they celebrated Diwali
With joy and lights galore.

Now many years later
On Dusshera, we celebrate
The defeat of the evil Raavana
By Lord Rama the Great.

Then begins Diwali
A festival so grand.
When family and friends gather
To celebrate hand in hand.

The children then get phuljaris
Which are so gleeful and fun.
As they sparkle, crackle, and shine
Like the rays of our glorious sun.

Diyas adorn the homes
And lights are lit in the streets.
Then comes all the feasting
On delicious foods and sweets.

With the help of parents and elders,
Fireworks light up the skies
To rejoice in Rama's greatness
In his victory over evil and lies.

We bow to the Goddess Lakshmi
For prosperity, joy, and wealth.
Create colored lotuses in rangoli
And pray for happiness and health.

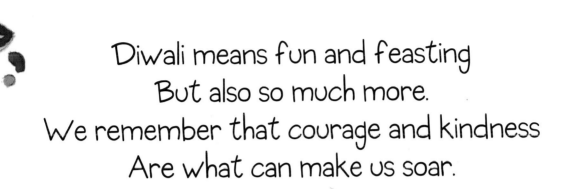

Diwali means fun and feasting
But also so much more.
We remember that courage and kindness
Are what can make us soar.

The strength and virtues of Rama
They teach us all the ways
To live with dharma and honor
In all of our nights and days.

Whether in the North
Or South, or East, or West
We may celebrate in different ways.
But they all make Diwali the best!

About the Author

Sana Hoda Sood is an Indian-American living in the Washington, DC metro area. Sana grew up celebrating the diversity of India through beautiful festivals such as Diwali, Eid, and Holi. Her cultural roots and Indian traditions are very close to her heart. As a new mother, Sana wanted her son to learn about them as well. While on maternity leave from her corporate career, she wrote *Diwali: A Cultural Adventure* to introduce her son, Aarish, to a vibrant aspect of his heritage. This is her first children's book, and has been illustrated in stunning watercolors by her mother, Rubina Hoda.